LOOP HOLE

Saurabh D Ingalkar

BlueRose ONE.com
Stories Matter
NewDelhi • London

BLUEROSE PUBLISHERS
India | U.K.

BlueRose ONE.com
Stories Matter
NewDelhi • London

For permissions requests or inquiries regarding this publication, please contact:

BLUEROSE PUBLISHERS
www.BlueRoseONE.com
info@bluerosepublishers.com
+91 8882 898 898
+4407342408967

ISBN: 978-93-7018-281-3

Cover design: Yash Singhal
Typesetting: Namrata Saini

First Edition: September 2025

MU

METHODICAL
UNIVERSE

INTRODUCTION

Strolling in the streets of Mumbai for 28 years, Saurabh unintentionally discovered the path to the world of writing and created his **debut Nomics** called **"Loophole"**. Saurabh Ingalkar is a fiction-based romantic, horror & sci-fi writer and for the past six years he has diligently written many stories with a motive to amuse and motivate readers to believe that

"Imagination is the best form of motion pictures that you can ever produce."

He is a young, aspiring wordsmith who started his journey as a writer from blogging his ingenuity into sentences in 2018. While completing his Post-Graduation in Integrated Marketing and Advertising in 2017, he desired to be a Social Media Marketer, but after an inspiring creative breakthrough and a certain turn of events, he decided to be an expressive writer and share with the world what his mind has abstracted. From there on, Saurabh turned from an amazing Content Writer to an astonishing Script Writer and Sr. Copywriter for various Bollywood celebrities. He now portrays the role of a Writer for U.S. story lovers in an audio series-based company and is finding the right place to celebrate and showcase his talent in the industry.

Saurabh stumbled upon this hooking concept of **"Loophole"** by questioning a simple thought - "Why does India lag behind when it comes to a sci-fi superhero story?" He wishes to write stories that inspire and engage the young audience in a way the foreign creators of caped crusaders did. Saurabh's only motive for creating this piece of art is to proudly represent Indian writers to the international world. The character **"Loophole"** and its story are solely his creation for all kinds of present and upcoming generations.

"Loophole" is Saurabh's debut Nomics and his vision to create a remarkable series out of it. Saurabh lives with his family of four and is currently working on the next part of **"Loophole"**. You can stalk him on his Instagram page **thespians_talent** and read his many amazing stories on his website **www.lovelaughlookout.wordpress.com**. Feel free to drop a question about his Nomics in the mail. **sourabhingalkar@yahoo.com**

The book "Loophole" offers a powerful exploration through the eyes of a child, unraveling deep-rooted conflicts with parents that make the narrative both intense and heartbreaking. The tension is skillfully built, laced with a subtle sense of mystery that surrounds each argument, keeping readers thoroughly engaged. As the story unfolds with unexpected twists and turns, it reaches an electrifying point where the unique child transforms into a fresh and fascinating superheroic being—delivering a thrilling, edge-of-the-seat experience. The story strikes a fine balance between realism and fiction, making it both believable and imaginative.

The writing style is immersive, with vivid descriptions that brilliantly capture the ever-shifting emotional landscape. Dialogues are strong and purposeful, effectively driving the plot forward. Overall, this sci-fi narrative is compelling and well-structured, injecting a wave of freshness and excitement into the superhero genre.

BlueRose Publishers

"If you don't let things happen the way they are meant to be, then whatever happens will always feel unnatural."

-Saurabh Ingalkar

Welcome to the world of **NOMICS – Novel-like read, comic-like feel.** Nomics is a new genre of reading that I invented for readers and story lovers like you. As a baby reader I always wondered if novels had some pictures that explained the scene better or helped me imagine the character more accurately, just like the way the writer did while portraying it. But then again, a picture in a book is often presumed to be a comic or a book not for avid readers, isn't it? I beg to differ; a picture could speak a thousand words. (That's a few thousand off my chest). Otherwise, how can a painting tell you stories? **Every form of art has its way of reaching our hearts. We just need to unlock the gate and greet it with open arms. That's why it is called "heART".**

Nomics is a new art style that not only helps readers understand the story better but also connects them with the world of pure imagination. This way they not only feel the story but also become a part of it. Nomics is a fresh way of making people fall in love with books and enjoy the world of imagination with a hint of support from the art of sight. Every sketch you cross paths with is handcrafted by me to make you see what I saw while writing this epic sci-fi saga. So, enjoy the world of Nomics as it's just the beginning…

CONTENTS

CHAPTER 1

The Demise of Love

(November 26th, 2024. 4:00 PM)

I was 10 when my parents split up. It never occurred to me "Why?" I never saw them fighting, yelling, cursing at each other before, like they did on that day.

(Mid-afternoon at J.J. Street, row house 102, Mumbai, India. Dave Family)

In the late afternoon, after school, my dad came rushing through the door in a fit of anger and distress. My mother and I were doing homework at the dining table in the kitchen. As he entered, he bellowed my mother's name once. Mom replied in a sweet, tender voice,

"In the kitchen."

He barged in and was about to yell, I could tell but feeling my presence in the room, he kept quiet. My mother heard his indignant footsteps and saw his trembling fist. There was a deep silence in the room for a minute. Dad continuously stared at mom in rage.

She felt something was wrong but to avoid a scene in front of me she kept quiet too. She asked me to go upstairs. I didn't argue as I was tired of studying. I quietly went to my room. A minute later, I heard dad shouting at mom for something. I wanted to investigate the matter so I thought of eavesdropping.

"How dare you do this?" my dad yelled in great anger and chagrin.

"Do what?" mom asked gently.

"Don't act innocent in front of me."

Saying that, he threw a file on the table in front of her.

"I found this in your lab while going through something."

At this moment, my mom started sweating nervously and broke eye contact with him. She marched towards the hall as she tried to avoid him.

"I...I don't know... I don't know what you are talking about," she fumbled.

Her eyes were lost somewhere and her voice sounded tense, as if her secret was out.

"Just because you gave him birth doesn't give you the right to tamper with his life Maya. I won't let this happen," dad warned her.

I never saw him so angry. He was so furious and angry that his wheatish skin was glowing red. His veins popped through his forehead. It was just a matter of time before he burst into flames like a real dragon. Yet he patiently waited for my mom's answer. Suddenly, my mom felt confident and relaxed.

"Oh really! And what will you do?"

She questioned with an attitude. There was a weird smirk on her face that I had never seen before. The one you possess when you have three aces in your hand at a table.

Irked, my father said, *"I will never let him see your filthy face ever again; I will take him so far away that your shadow will also yearn for him."*

He marched towards my room when my mother stopped him.

"No, wait! You can't take him." Her eyes became watery.

"He is my child too. My creation. You cannot just take him away from me." Frustrated and helpless, she said, *"I am sorry… I know I should have told you but…"* She sobbed.

Her mood kept changing like flicking through TV channels. From angry to frustrated, from helpless to careless, from pleading to owning every inch of the room. It was bemusing. My father said some things, my mother acted inversely. It was all too bizarre and pointless to me but one thing was quite clear - that the skirmish was about me. I was there on the staircase, listening to everything they were arguing about but didn't understand a bit of it.

Have you ever been one of those guys in high school who stand out among all, who is different, and being "different" felt like a curse? Well, I have been that guy. I looked the same as all but was different inside. My school days used to start with fights on the bus and end with me being in a dumpster, upside down. Not a single day do I remember coming home without crying. My mom always used to tell me that I was her 'miracle of science'; and that it took me 11 months to get out of her womb and the following month to develop my brain. She said that I was declared brain dead when I was born but after an hour my heart started beating. I was alive. It had to be a miracle. Even though my brain worked half my age, it never bothered my parents. They loved me a lot, with all the faults in my stars.

Anyways, after four hours of pointless and somewhat hideous argument, my father left the house, slamming the door. I fell asleep on the staircase while hearing all this nonsense until the loud slam of the door woke me up. The house was quiet. The silence felt good for a moment but I had to go down. I was hungry. I slowly came down step-by-step, trying to maintain the peace. The house was so eerily silent, I could hear every tick of the 'Hello Kitty' clock echoing through the stillness. As I reached down the staircase, I called my mom but I didn't get any answer. I slowly moved towards the kitchen wondering that she might be preparing for dinner but the kitchen had no sign of her. My books were scattered on the table under a file named *"Project Guiser"*. I picked the file and started going through it, but unfortunately, my puny brain couldn't understand a word in it. I kept it as it was on the table, trying to maintain the peace around the house. Suddenly, I heard a sound coming from the hall. I ran towards it. And I saw MOM. A great, joyful smile was visible on my face. She was sitting on her favorite chair near the window, her eyes staring upwards at a certain point as if she was in a deep thought.

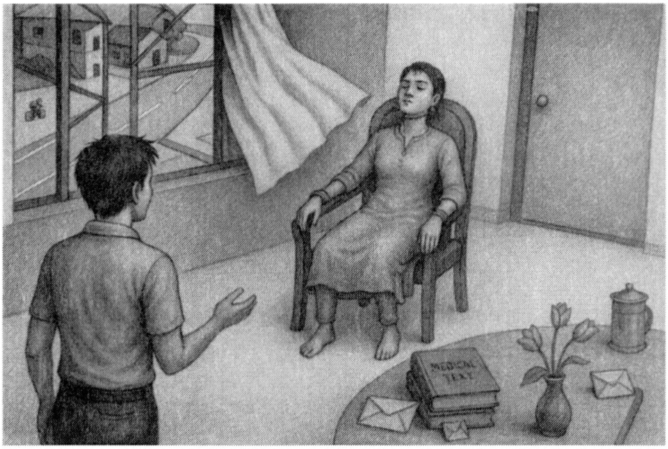

I saw my dad drive away from the window. He drove away faster than usual and didn't even wave back at me like he used to do, always. It was devastating for me. It almost felt like he was not my dad. I turned towards my mom and asked her numerous questions.

"Where did dad go, mamma? Where did he go? Why were you guys fighting, mamma? Was it because of me? Was I bad?"

I sobbed a little bit. I didn't like the idea of me being the reason for my parents' fight. A tear rolled down my cheek as I comforted her.

"I am sorry! I promise I will be a good boy both of you will be proud of."

I sat down on my knees, leaning my head on her lap for a while.

"Is the dinner ready yet?"

I asked after a while, in an irresistible voice.

Neither of my questions were answered. She just kept staring at the ceiling continuously. I noticed a strange line-like mark on her neck. I didn't know what it was. I thought it was some kind of aging problem so I neglected it and I shook her to get her attention. As soon as I did, her head dropped down, looking straight at the ground now. I got up and took a step back in a jolt. She was unresponsive, which scared me a bit. Even though a child, I knew what this meant, and I was not ready for it. I slowly moved towards her, calling her, hoping to get back an answer.

"MOM?... Mom!!"

But she didn't move even a bit. I grabbed her finger. My eyes were wet, I called her again, praying that this would turn out to be one of her pranks which she used to do on me.

"Mom…M…MOM," I said, and sat on my knees holding her fingers and crying.

I kept my head on her lap and closed my eyes, hoping she would brush my hair with her hands and will call my name. At that moment, I didn't want anything more than that.

As I was resting my head on my dead mom's lap, I felt a rage inside me. I was angry, devastated, and way out of granting forgiveness to whomsoever did this. It was my dad. It had to be him. Who else could be so mad to do something like this to her? A moment ago, they were fighting and the next thing I knew, was that my mom had died. I ran towards the garage, took out my bicycle which my mom had gifted me last summer and followed my father. The bicycle was too slow to catch up with a car but I knew where he would have gone to, at this time. Where all scientists go. To his lab, in VPRO *(Vacuum and astro-Physics Research Organization)*. Out of the city. Somewhere, Nowhere.

It was just a mile away from the town. Being his son, getting in wasn't a problem but there were no guards at the gate or inside the building, which made things smoother. I saw his car in the parking lot. I knew he might be in there. I left my cycle and ran inside towards his lab.

I needed my answers. I wanted to know why he killed her. What happened back there? They both loved each other. How can he do this? I was running like a wild dog behind a garbage truck, reckless and irritated. My eyes were wet but my fist was tight and there were lots of questions in my mind. I was so angry that I didn't even realize that the red emergency alarms were buzzing loudly, and there was no one in the building. Least bothered, I ran into his lab. Nobody was in there, neither in his lab nor in the entire facility. The entire building was evacuated. And the reason was right in front of me - an unstable wormhole which was as big as the clock on Big Ben and was growing rapidly. Dad had told me that he was working on one and how it could change the history of mankind. I was so proud of my father, until today. The wormhole started growing bigger and bigger. It started sucking everything in my vicinity. I ran for my life but the force was too strong for a 10-year-old kid. I grabbed the doorknob tightly but my legs levitated towards it. The force was getting so strong that I started losing my grip, and I did. I almost entered the wormhole.

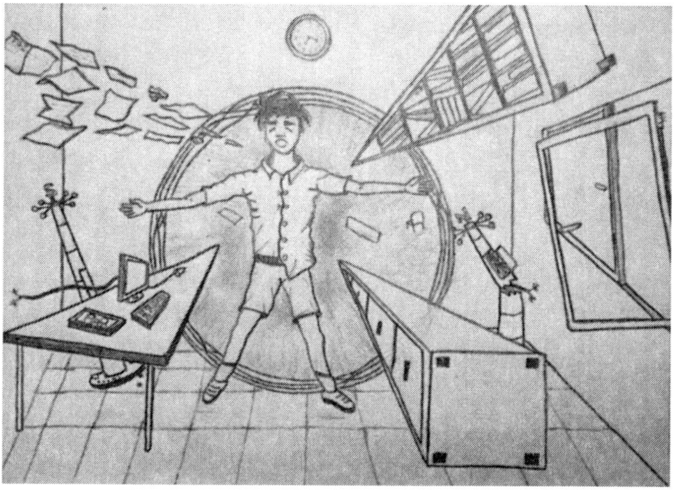

I was on the edge of its opening. I closed my eyes and started screaming

"DAAAAD!!!!"

All of a sudden, my fingers touched something; I didn't know what, but the very next second the wormhole exploded. The explosion was so big that it destroyed the entire building. I was sent flying through walls and doors until I fell on the ground. My entire body felt like it was being pierced by thousands of needles. I was badly hurt and was lying down under a huge ceiling slab, hoping my father would come and pick me up. There was no one around but my bicycle in bits and pieces. I blacked out.

CHAPTER 2

Agastya Dave

(6 hours ago, at the Vacuum and astro-Physics Research Organization's headquarters.)

(November 26th, 2024. 2:00 PM)

"15 years! 15 years of intense diligence will pay off today,"

My partner NAT said in a satisfied and happy voice.

"Yes. We are about to create history my old friend. Just a few more tests and the first-ever stable wormhole will be ready to peek beyond galaxies," I said with joy and pride as we both were working in the lab.

NAT and I have been friends for a very long time, even before we became renowned scientists. I was an expert in astrophysics and NAT was an exceptional theoretical physicist. His study in the subject of wormholes was profound and staggering. Even though I was his senior, it never affected our relationship. Our friendship was so sturdy that even our children were BFFs. We both stood up for each other on every occasion, ace or atrocious; we never left each other's side. He was not only my beloved crony but my neighbor, my mentor, my child's godfather and my family.

I respected him a lot because of the agonizing struggle he had been through. The man's life had been a living hell before he met me. Tragedy does not seem to have a different address to go to. Still NAT faced every plight in his life with a smile on his face, and hope in his heart for a better tomorrow. He always used to quote:

"Integrity of a person grows with the tragedy he or she faces in life."

Just a year ago he lost his son *Siddhant* and wife *Pallavi* in a house fire. Since then, we have been closer to him than ever. My son Advik was more attached to him than me. Advik was very depressed after losing his only friend in his life. Thanks to NAT for helping him recover from it, keeping his own melancholy aside. In a way, both of them healed each other. NAT needed Advik more than he could have imagined.

But now everything was going to be fine as this breakthrough would make both of us the most successful scientists in the entire world and make human life much more advanced and easier. Our project "Limitless Occurrence of Over-through Portals" or as we like to call it "L.O.O.P" has the capability to make transportation easy and explore the universe in one click. This would be a window to discover every life form beyond Earth spread out in every universe. With just one click, people would be able to go anywhere in the world without spending hours of time on traveling.

"How are those artificial magnetic poles coming along Aggs?"

NAT asked me as he was in charge of this project because it was his idea. He used to call me "Aggs" as a short form of my name *"Agastya"*.

"The two poles are exactly identical to our Earth's poles, NAT. It will be ready to operate within an hour. Just minor changes and we will be able to set its radius according to our will," I replied while working on those two magnetic poles.

"Careful with it, those things are very important while creating a live wormhole. Even one minor fault and the

entire wormhole will collapse, sucking everything in until it explodes," NAT warned while working.

He was not wrong about it though. These poles were similar, yet a smaller version of North and South Poles of our Earth which created a magnetic field around us, generating a fake gravitational pull. This helps us to avoid getting lured inside the wormhole keeping it stable and resist its growth. I nodded as I worked on it.

"So how is Advik doing?" NAT asked. *"I heard he is being bullied a lot at school?"*

"Some days are rough on him but nothing that chocolates and a theme park can't handle. After all he is just a kid and kids tend to forget pain when they gain something they like."

I smirked, trying to hide my worry for my boy. As I was in my pool of brooding, I heard a phone ring. It was the director of VPRO asking for me. *"What does she want now?"* NAT asked in a funny way after my call ended. He had never really been fond of her. She always got in the way of how NAT wanted things. They had a cat and mouse kind of a relationship and I was the monkey in between.

"Just some file she left at Maya's Lab," I said as I was heading towards her lab.

"Oh okay, is Maya not here? Why doesn't she call her?" NAT curiously asked.

"She was, but earlier this afternoon she went home for Advik. She'll feed him now, make him do his homework, put him down for a nap and then return later today," I said while checking my phone and trying to call Maya.

"Hardcore mother, passionate career enthusiast - a rare combination these days," NAT said.

"Nah, not that rare in India," I said with a smile while leaving the lab. *"Will be back, don't start the funhouse without me."* Saying that I left for Maya's lab.

The genetic-engineering section was right above the astro-physics department. Intriguingly, her lab was right above ours. I casually went inside her lab and started looking for the file Director Raven had mentioned. Though the smell of the chemicals gave me discomfort, the creeps came from the glass cage she had in her lab; because as soon as I entered, the cage started banging and scratching from inside. It was soundproof, yet eerie. Whatever was inside it - was desperate to come out and feast on me. But I had no idea what it was. Even though it looked like glass, the cage was made with a solid material that could even withstand a nuclear holocaust. It was designed as a coded glass. Only the person who knew the code was able to see through it and access it; for the rest, it was a one-way mirror for self-admiration.

Anyway, I kept looking for the file all around the place. Maya was too private about her things, so I had to be careful about where everything exactly belonged. I saw a small cabinet in the corner of the room and thought of searching it. That's one of the obvious places where an organized woman would keep her files. I pulled out the bottom compartment after checking the two above it. There was a stack of files lined up one after the other alphabetically. I found what I was looking for but I observed an odd thing about those arranged files. A letter 'G' was missing from the stack which didn't make any sense as Maya was very organized and prudent about stuff like this. It was so unlike her to tabulate her files in such order and not notice that she was missing one. But then again, I thought she might have taken that file with her. So, giving no further thought to it, I pushed the drawer in or at least I tried to do so. But something was coming in its way. I shook the drawer a little bit to fit it right in, but it came out. As I tried to put it back in, I noticed an envelope peeking from the drawer's hollow compartment. It was taped on the inside of the compartment. I kept the drawer full of files aside and removed the envelope out of curiosity.

I had numerous thoughts in my mind before opening it.

What's in it? What's so secretive to keep it this hidden? Is she working on a clandestine project? Did Maya have an affair, and are there pictures in this envelope of her boyfriend and her? What's in this?

Curiosity crawled down from my head to my hands and I couldn't resist it but to open and see. I was relieved after seeing that it was just a file.

But when I looked closely, I noticed it was the same file that was missing from the file stack. The 'G' file called as 'Project Guiser'. But what was in that file so important that it had to be kept this hidden, even from me. I don't recall Maya uttering the name 'Guiser' ever in front of me, when in fact, we share everything with each other.

This was beyond resistance now. I had to know what was in that file, which Maya never spoke of. This was something she never did. Secrecy was never her thing. *How come now?* I opened the file and could have never been more disappointed than ever before. I regretted opening it and wished it was her affair pics - that would have been better. But it was not. This thing was much bigger than a stupid liaison. My anger was over the edge now. Confrontation was the only solution for this problem. I furiously left the premises and hurried towards home.

CHAPTER 3

Go Slow – Agony Ahead

(Same day, early morning)

(Few hours before demise. Maya and Agastya drop Advik off at his school bus and watch him go, until the bus disappeared on its next turn. Maya weeps a bit as Agastya holds her in.)

(November 26th, 2024. 6:50 AM)

It was a new day again. I was standing outside on the porch with my parents waiting for the school bus to arrive. It was the first day after Diwali vacation. My eyes were on the road but my heart was in resistance. I had no intention of going back to the school, not since Siddhant *bhaiya* left me. He was Uncle NAT's son and like an elder brother to me. That's why I called him "*bhaiya*", an elder, caring, loving and protective brother. His death left me hollow inside. The grief was far beyond understanding because he was the only one in the school who nurtured the true me, neglecting all my shortcomings.

Dad was running late for work today, yet he stood with me and Mom. I loved him even more when he did something like that. I was holding my mom's hand and I squeezed it tightly as I saw the school bus arriving. I started getting nervous and my legs started to tremble as the distance between me and the bus narrowed. The fear of being around the people who neglected my existence was at its peak. Mom noticed my frazzled and strange behaviour as I took two steps behind in distress. The bus stopped in front of us welcoming me to experience yet another 'worst day of my life'. We, as in Siddhant *bhaiya* and I, named it 'BROM', Bus-Rage-Operating-Monster. I missed it.

As the bus stopped, I noticed some scary stares from the windows. It made me uncomfortable and awkward. I hid behind my mom to avoid it.

"Advik! What happened? Come out now... Come on...Your bus is here" Mom said in a concerned but compelling voice.

"I don't wanna go brom," I said in a very low voice adding a little sobbing to it for better sound effects.

"What? Why?" Mom asked out of concern and surprise.

"No one likes me there", I answered in a soft, depressed voice and looked at the eyes peeking out the windows. It felt like I was looking in the dark abyss and all of a sudden, multiple eyes glowing red from lust or hunger to rip me apart started popping up one by one. Mom saw what I was feeling - a sense of fear, embarrassment and

anxiety, all together at the same time. She was concerned for my well-being but she gathered her perturbed feelings to make me feel better. She went down on her knees and leveled her eyes with me.

"Advik! Look at me", she said lifting my chin up.

"No one, and I mean no one will like you… unless you like yourself." She spoke those words out of pure love and with some next-level confidence which I craved.

"Do you like yourself?" she asked.

"Uh ha", I made a sound and nodded.

"Then don't you dare care what others feel about you. Love yourself! Until you know how to love yourself, you won't be able to love others. Always remember, Love starts with an 'I' and ends with a 'U'. That is why we say I - LOVE - YOU! So, will you love YOU now?" She continued to end with a question.

"Yes! I will love myself."

I threw a smile at her that came right from my heart and I hugged her tight.

"But I will always LOVE YOU more, cheeku", she expressed.

We let go of the hug and I boarded the bus. The bus moved as she looked at me till I was invisible for her eyes. Later, dad took her in as she sobbed a little. As the tires rolled around the ground, the unknown fear and distress kicked in again. The confidence my mom gave me was lost in a minute as I turned around and saw the shunned faces staring at me. I was standing near the door baffled. I turned back to the door to get down but then I noticed it was already in motion. There was no other choice for me but to pass through these people. I wasn't scared for no reason; I knew what was coming next. Every new day was worse than yesterday. It was bearable when Siddhant *bhaiya* was around but since he bailed on me, the school had turned into a nightmare.

As I went through, everyone denied my presence. The few rows in the front used to always be occupied by the teacher's pets. Usually they debated about scientific possibilities or technological advancements, but today they were studying quietly for some test. Behind them were the mixed breed goons of disgust, attitude, wealthy pride, introverts and some good people who were scared to do the right thing. We called them *the bagpiper rats.*

Our seat used to be among them but today it was all taken. I didn't have the guts to ask anyone to move, so I walked further. The last row of the bus was always taken by the group of tyrannical kids who I was scared of, a lot. Not just me, but everyone. No one used to dare to sit in their seats even in their absence. I stopped as I reached in front of them. They were busy with their nonsense but they noticed my intruding presence. They all stared at me with a rebellious and seething look. I turned around and looked away trying to not get in their way. A while later, they continued with their chaotic behaviour. I was standing still when I noticed an empty seat right in front of them. At first, I hesitated to settle there, but then I thought that I wasn't getting in anyone's way or spoiling the fun. So, I took off my bag and was about to settle my butt down when someone from behind poured water all over the seat.

It was obviously not a mistake. Only a fool would see it like that. I didn't dare to even look who did it. I stood with my bag in hand thinking 'What now?' No one wanted to share a seat with me and the only single seat was now a half an hour water joy ride with three more stops in between. My legs were hurting because of the heavy bag I carried. I sat down on the floor shamelessly with no regard whatsoever. I heard laughter. People threw paper rockets at me. I was unable to do anything but to put my head down and shed a tear remembering mom.

Forty-five minutes passed by. I was walking down the hallway towards the classroom. I kept my head down to neglect any eye contact but I noticed that everyone was looking at me as I passed by them. Except Siddhant *bhaiya*, I had one more friend who loved my company; *Kartik*. But he too left me out of peer pressure.

The reason behind people acting strange around me was not just my dumbness but also their stupidity. They all believed that Siddhant *bhaiya*'s death was caused by our friendship. It was assumed that I was the black cat in their life. That's why everyone made a distance, for their own sake. Siddhant *bhaiya* was two grades above me and a very popular and charming student of the school. Good in studies, smart in athletics. Girls' favourite, guys' dude, yet he used to hang around with me more than with anyone else. Maybe that was also one of the many reasons they disliked me. They envied me before him; they banished me after him, but no one felt any sorrow or pity for me.

Anyways, as I entered the class, I sat at the very end corner of the row, alone. *Kartik* was now in the herd of popular kids in class. There was a time when he used to sit with me every day but everything had changed. He didn't even notice my presence, or maybe he did, but he didn't care much. That hurt me every single day giving me a sense of betrayal.

The lectures began one after another. Soon it was time for a break, everyone left their seats and got mixed with their favourite people. It was chaos all around; people running, fighting, drawing on the board, sharing meals, laughing, giggling, probably at me. Even I wanted to experience the feeling of sharing food and show them all how delicious my mom's food was. But I knew that no one would taste food from my tiffin box, in fact, if I even tried to join them, they might as well just leave, and I didn't want that. I didn't want to be a fun spoiler for someone. So I quietly ate by myself. *"More for me,"* I said and made my peace with it.

Today was still a pretty calm day, but that's because *Kalpak*, *Aasim* and *Krushika* were absent from school. Who are they? They are my personal bullies. Just like people have personal bodyguards, I like to have personal bullies chasing me through the entire school. No one else but me is who they are always after. Want to hang someone on the wall? Me. Want to lock someone in a toilet? Me. Want to throw someone's bag out of the bus? Mine. Want to create a fuss and blame it on someone? Always me. I was their only favourite thing to do. In fact, they enjoyed schooling because of me. They might be missing me today. I hope they die.

The day ended pretty well today. I even got a seat on the bus, on my way back home. I smiled as I got off the bus and saw my home. It was locked though. Neither mom nor dad had come early today. Usually, they don't even come during the day but because of my nanny being on vacation, they wanted at least one of them to be present with me. I got in with a duplicate key that mom had given me, just in case. Home alone is the sweetest thing to be. You can do whatever you want. I removed my shoes and threw them on the rack. I ran towards the TV, dropping all my school accessories on the way and binge-watched my favourite cartoon. An hour later, mom came in calling my name. I was asleep on the couch in front of the TV. Her warm comforting touch woke me up. We had lunch together in the kitchen and later sat down to do homework.

CHAPTER 4

Leap Year

(10 years later at a secret base vessel. Somewhere in the middle of South Atlantic Ocean.)

(May 18th, 2035. 12:15 PM)

For the first time, sound travelled faster than the light could reach my eyes. Everything seemed to be blurry and foggy. The place was not what I could recall. My vision was foggy, yet I was able to see some blurry movements. It felt like I was deep inside the sea and was gazing at people moving inside a submarine.

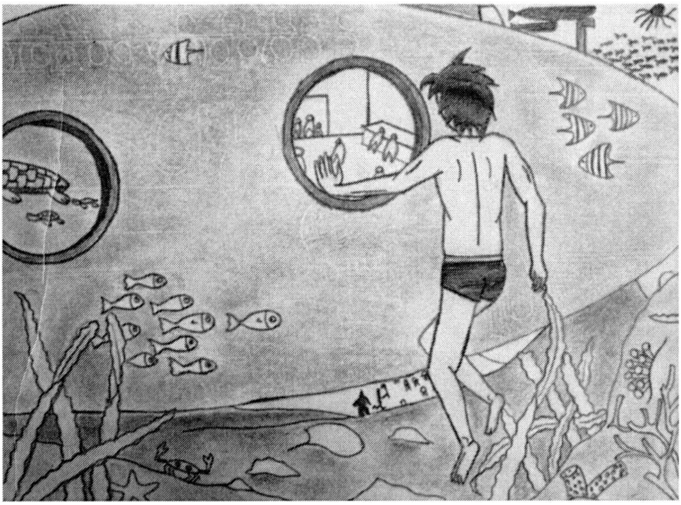

I noticed being surrounded by ticklish things. It seemed like algae and kelp. Everything felt dizzy and dreamy. I was enjoying it until something stung me from behind. That sting broke my reverie. My hallucination took a break to witness reality. There was no sea, algae or kelp that I was surrounded with, but wires and tubes poked deep inside my body in a containment tube. The tube was filled with chemicals and various other kinds of stuff that made the liquid look greenish.

"Heart rate stable," one said.

"Brain waves normalizing," the other guy from the corner quoted.

"Dr Shelly, I need your expertise here,"

The guy standing right in front of me in a white coat stated when a woman walked gracefully toward him.

It seemed like her presence was of great importance in the room. I was scared and felt suffocated. Who wouldn't be? And I was just a 10-year-old child. The mere thought of me drowning made me furious. I started banging the confinement from inside for some attention. Everyone looked at me except Shelly. Dr Shelly seemed like a mid-aged, arrogant and dominating woman who had nothing to do with me but science. She didn't glance at me once. Her ignorance made me hoppin' mad. I looked around for someone to step up, but no one dared to move a muscle because of her dread. She smirked and got back to work. I kept on bashing each one harder than before.

Annoyed by me, Shelly walked close to me and rudely said,

"Quit banging. That thing is bulletproof. It won't break. So stop clamouring and let us work, it's for your own good."

Saying that, she turned back and started walking. I, like every other kid in the world, had only one rule 'tit for tat': in this case, 'ignorance-for-ignorance'. I kept banging the tube until I heard a cracking sound. Shelly slowly turned back as she was leaving. Everything, everybody stopped still.

All eyes were on the crack as it was growing. The room was silent as a womb. The crack on the tube kept growing all around and all of a sudden, it stopped at one point. Everyone felt relieved except me. But a few seconds later, the tube fissured and threw me out with force. The wires and tubes jabbed inside me were still attached.

Seeing me lying on the ground, naked and unstable, Shelly hit the giant red button. That red light censored my consciousness and reminded me of my incomplete vengeance. The rage that once ignited me before the blast came rushing back, raw and unrelenting. The day when I lost everything. With mixed emotions of anger, threat, devastation, anxiety, loneliness, loss and a whole other level of darkness, I got up. I was confused and was feeling a bit dizzy. I felt tall and heavy. My arms felt strong and my stomach felt hungry. My vision went stygian and all of a sudden, I was alone in the dark space, abandoned and exiled. At that very moment, I saw a bright streak of gleam coming right at me. The gleam thumped my solar. I felt a massive pain. I screamed till my throat went dry.

"Ma'am, the subject is unstable," a guy near me said.

"Kill the energy source now," Shelly ordered.

"But ma'am, that will kill him," the girl nearby showed her concern.

"Shut up, Kirti. I know what I am doing. Just do as I said," Shelly shouted furiously, after which the

young girl Kirti ran out of the door without getting in Shelly's eye.

Shelly's voice screamed in my ears and tempted my patience. After that, my anger had no limits. I sensed powerful dark energy coming out of me. After the throbbing *"imaginary"* encounter with the gleams, I was back in front of Shelly, floating. My eyes went dark and my body possessed numerous small and big holes, with every hole holding 'n' number of galaxies and stars in it. It looked like a circular window to space. The biggest one was on my solar where the light had hit me but it wasn't deep and dark like the others. It glowed like the sun.

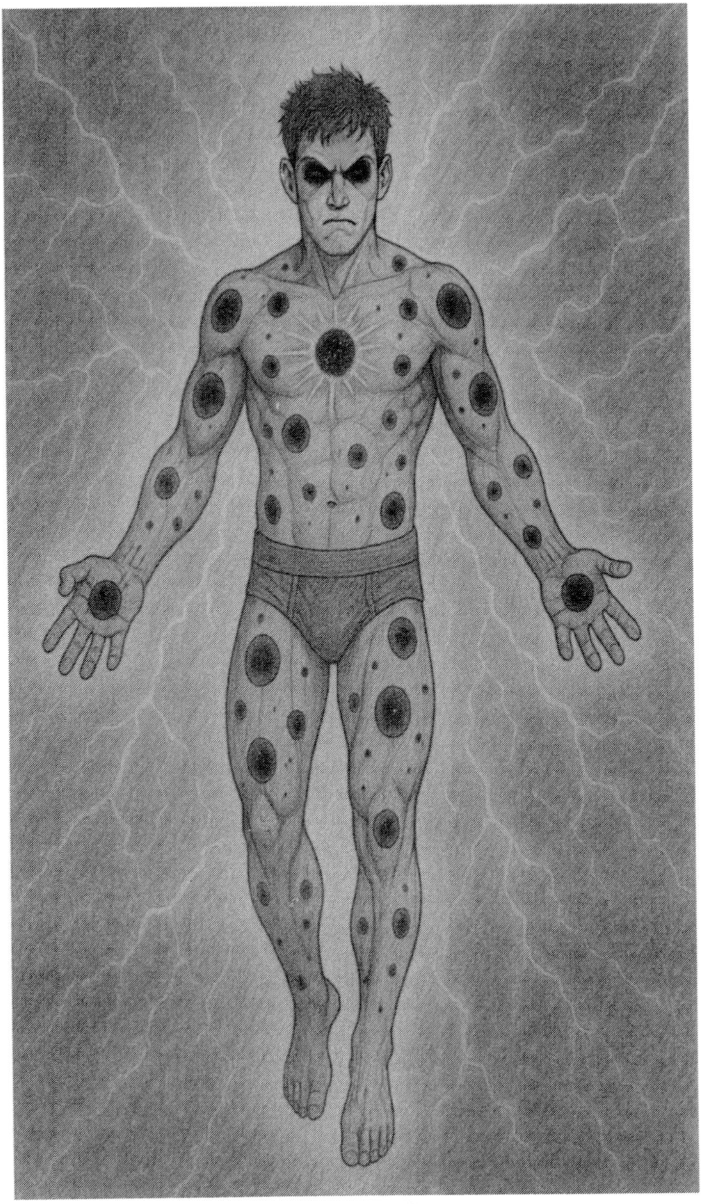

Detaching all the wires and tubes, I slowly floated towards Shelly, with only one intention, to kill the one who tried to kill me. She was shocked and scared, and was slowly taking one step back at a time. Out of the blue, few black SWAT stood between me and her with guns, batons and tasers. I stopped to address the situation. But Shelly felt that I got scared. She felt relieved. I didn't want her to feel that.

"What are you waiting for? Kill him," Shelly ordered the SWATs furiously.

Before anybody could even move a muscle, I looked at Shelly with rogue eyes and raised my hand, aiming her. A wormhole opened right below her feet and she flushed down, screaming. It wasn't me, but somehow it still felt like me. I had no control over my actions anymore. It was as if I was watching a scene from the movies in a big theater. I had no other option but to observe what was happening.

After what happened with Shelly, everyone was shocked and scared. Even the SWATs hesitated to attack me, yet they aimed at me. The baton SWAT attacked me first from my left side but before he could reach me, I grabbed him by his neck and lifted him 6ft above the ground. He struggled to break my grip on him as everyone just stood there, petrified. I threw him towards the right wall, but before he could hit the bricks, I opened a hole right behind him. The guy disappeared into a dark abyss, screaming his lungs out. But the wormhole was still open and under control. The taser guy tried to shock me by catching me off guard, but before his tasers reached me, I opened up another hole in front of me and its adjoining hole behind the gun SWATs. As a result, the gun SWATs were brutally tased.

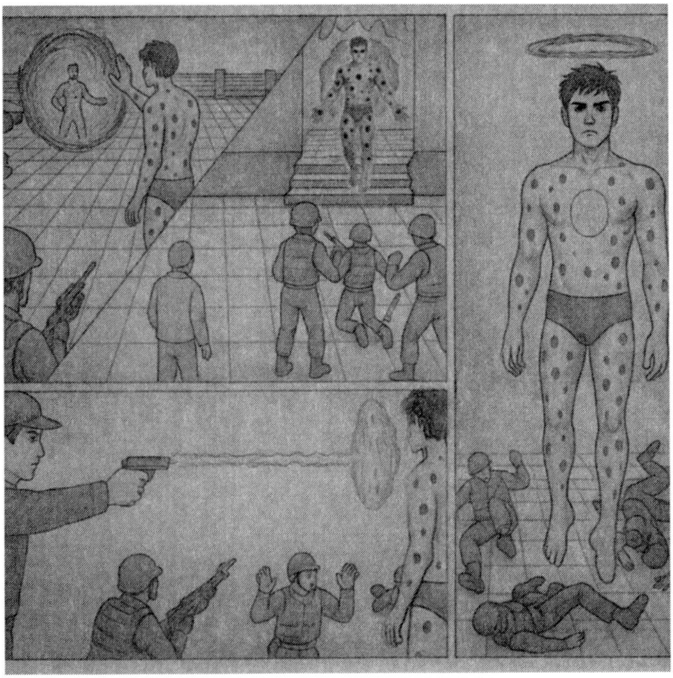

Seeing all the SWATs vanquished, the taser SWAT feared my dominating presence. As I slowly floated towards him, he started to tremble. His legs froze and his eyes started shedding tears, as if saying to spare him. I went closer to him and opened up another hole right above him. At first he got confused. He looked up at the wormhole for a few seconds. It was the size of a ceiling fan. It was stable and beautiful. Mesmerized by the beauty of space, he never noticed what was coming for him through it. A hard, cold, and heavy body fell down from the hole, right on the head of the SWAT guard breaking his bones, the sound of which echoed in the silent room. Everyone saw the body that fell from the sky. It was the very first guy who tried to attack me with a baton, now frozen hard and cold-blooded as if he was buried a thousand feet under the ice. The entire SWAT team was defeated and unconscious within minutes.

Everyone feared me in that room. Some collapsed, some ran away, some stood still in shock. All of a sudden, I heard a person calling my name.

"ADVIK, stop."

Somehow, the voice sounded familiar. I turned to see who it could be and I was shocked to my very core. The wormhole on my body started to disappear one by one. And the one that I created in thin air vanished like a sinking hole at the shore of the beach, as soon as my feet touched the ground. My eyes looked normal, but a tear rolled down my cheek as soon as I saw that person.

CHAPTER 5

The Falling Star (Part 1)

(Somewhere in the midst of the Pacific Ocean. Right after the incident on the secret base vessel.)

(May 18th, 2035. 12:40 PM)

A mysterious hole appeared 50ft above the sea level and a woman fell down from it screaming her throat out. A big splash of water was visible as she sank into the cold, wild sea. After touching a depth of 30ft, she swam up to the surface. It was Shelly, who was catching her breath after a diabolical encounter with Advik.

Short of breath and scared to her core, she pulled herself together and tried to figure out her whereabouts.

"I need to be paid more,"

She joked about what had happened to her, to comfort herself. But nothing made her feel better as she realized that the situation had gotten worse than ever.

Wherever she looked, wherever her sight reached, everything was wet-blue. No ships, no sand, but a cold breeze above her head and unknown creatures below her feet, with no one else to witness this but her. Shelly was shaken to her core but not a single tear came out of her strong eyes. No doubt she was scared, but without panicking or wasting her energy, she pulled herself together. It did take her time to process everything as all of this happened in a snap. After a while, she pulled her phone out and tried to contact the base but her phone was wet-dead. Shelly got frustrated seeing that.

"I knew I should have bought the waterproof one," Shelly expressed, splashing the water in anger.

"Oh wait, my watch...My watch can help me track down the nearest human heartbeat. Oh... THANK YOU HINT,"

She screamed in joy and used her watch for the desired purpose. The watch showed a holographic map of her surroundings.

"Let's see...hmmm...135 heartbeats around me...fish, fish, fish, octopus, fish, fish, fish...Aha! ...80 beats per minute...there's my savior...Northeast. Fuck! 25 miles away!!" she screamed in great shock and disappointment.

Shelly had no other choice but to swim all the way till there. Anyways, it was not beneficial to stay at the same spot unless she wished to die in the jaws of a shark. She started swimming towards that direction and kept her eyes open for dangers as well as opportunities. After three hours of striving to reach somewhere, Shelly got tired and was losing hope of surviving. Her hands started to feel numb and she couldn't feel her legs either. She was struggling to keep herself up and awake. Her eyes slowly started to get heavy and so did her body. She knew that if she didn't stay awake she would drown forever without anyone knowing about it. But she was too helpless and too tired to struggle. Shelly thought that it was better to close her eyes and let everything go, than to brawl and make death more difficult. As she was about to accept her death, a ray of life struck her eyes.

A rescue buoy was floating half a mile away from her. It might have accidentally fallen from a passing ship. Whatever it might have been, it was nothing less than God's own hand that came to her rescue. Seeing the buoy, Shelly felt relieved. She gathered whatever energy she had left in her and swam towards it slowly. Her left hand didn't respond much as the shoulder was sore and swollen. Swimming with one hand, she barely made a difference. But the will to live kept her alive, awake and energetic. After some time, she reached the rescue buoy, held it tight and anchored its rope around herself. The buoy was too small to fit a grown woman, so instead of climbing on it, she let the buoy carry half her body weight. Dr. Shelly was too tired to do anything anymore. As she leaned onto the rescue buoy, she became unconscious.

CHAPTER 6

What Concerns?

(Right after the battle on the secret base vessel.)

(May 18th, 2035. 12:45 PM)

I was shocked. I was shaken to my very core. *How could it be?* A tear rolled down my cheek but a smile also appeared from nowhere. It was my MOM standing right at the door calling my name.

But how was it possible? I saw her lying dead on her chair, then how could she be standing in front of me?

Nevertheless, least bit bothered about anything else I ran towards her like a lost pup in the wilderness. Stumbling; falling; happy. I hugged her tightly and cried out loud like a child. I didn't care about my nakedness or the fact that we had an audience. I cried till my heart felt relieved. Her hands brushed my hair backward and rubbed my back until I felt better. But it didn't calm me down at all. In fact, I started shedding tears with more intensity as if a long unfulfilled desire had finally come alive. It felt like I had been waiting for that to happen for almost thousands of years. It was indescribable. I kept hugging her tightly, each time more strongly than before, when my mom asked me to bring back Dr Shelly. It was peculiar to hear her ask that than asking about the well-being of her own damn child. I noticed that she hadn't even hugged me back as I clung to her tightly. But I assumed that she might be as shocked as I was.

I finally let go of the embrace to wipe my running nose and my tears with my hand, and replied,

"But how? I don't even know where I sent her."

My mom kept asking me to gain a grasp on my powers or at least try to remember where I transported her but I kept denying, as I didn't have any clue about how and where she was. That eerie experience was nothing more than a vicious and grotesque scene from that Mortal Kombat game that I was chained to watch.

Her constant nagging kept making me feel guilty, anxious and ashamed of myself. She saw me lose control and paused as I still tried to find peace and help her in any way that was possible, until she touched my cheek with her hand and told me that she would help me control my abilities and find Dr. Shelly. Her touch felt like heaven to me, like a block of ice on a 1,000-degree Fahrenheit day. I held her hand that was against my cheek and noticed something unusual. Holding her hand felt different. It was rough and firm.

All of a sudden everything changed when I touched her watch by mistake. I took a step back in shock as soon as I saw my mom turn into someone else. It was some kind of technical glitch, a holographic hoax, which kept flickering on and off.

"Uncle NAT!" I expressed in anger and disbelief. NAT, shocked and terrified, tried to reverse what happened by fiddling with his watch.

Uncle NAT was a south-Indian guy in his 50s. He was an expert scientist and a smart human being. His intelligence and experience could be seen through his semi-bald head and golden spectacles that he carried with confidence. A well-mannered being who carried himself well in formals, marking himself as a true gentleman, he was equally feared and respected by many. He was known to work with my dad in VPRO. NAT was actually acronym for his name which he never told anyone, I don't know why.

"Advik! Wait…I…I can explain",

NAT said while he tried to disarm the watch with his trembling hands.

"No, you can't", I replied in anger.

"How dare you defile the one I loved the most?"

Disappointed, my eyes turned murky again. My anger now had a channel, yet it was out of my control. The state of total seclusion in the abyss was yanking me into its depth yet again to witness something gruesome and atrocious.

"Where is my mother? What have you done with her?"

My voice sounded deeper and deeper with every word that came out of my mouth.

"W… we don't have her Advik. No one can. I know it's hard for you to cope with your mother and father's death… but"

I opposed to what he said loudly. *"He is not dead - But he soon will be."*

I floated up in anger and disagreement as I saw them all fear for their lives again. I was once again this stroppy and contumacious being that manifested numerous wormholes which peaked far beyond galaxies like a loophole in the universe.

"He died Advik. The black hole that we both created slurped him in. I somehow saved myself but failed to save him. We…we tried… we tried to find him a lot but later we accepted his decease," NAT told me with regret, devastated.

"That's because you tried out of pity and not out of vengeance. He will pay for his crimes, and so will you."

My body slowly flew towards him like a flame to the moth.

"No. Wait!" NAT requested.

"I did all this to protect you Advik… and to bring back Shelly," he expressed his intentions.

I somehow stopped my body from moving. I don't know how, but I stopped; not because he told me to, not because his intentions were to protect me—and certainly not because he was my uncle. I stopped, because I didn't want to calm my thirst for vengeance on a simple pawn.

He was my dad's friend; wouldn't it be obvious that he would have been trying to protect him? I just wanted to see how long he could do that. I wanted my dad to face this new rage of mine first, so to waste it on NAT was a kaput. I paused to think about a few things. Although I might have the endowments of a god yet my heart was innocent and I knew what I did earlier with Shelly was not righteous. My mother, if she was here, would not have been happy with this kind of behaviour of mine, especially toward women. But what Shelly did deserved a punishment. That's why I didn't bring her back, but I gave a hint to uncle NAT about her whereabouts.

"You want Shelly? She sails with the forgotten now — no land, no light, just endless drowning. Keep searching... the sea is always hungry."

Saying that I disappeared from the lab through a wormhole like a magician in a box.

NAT became furious and marched towards his office. His gut was grinding for some reason, as fear, anxiety, tension, and anger cluttered his mind. His raging steps echoed through the corridor of the vessel that floated in the middle of the ocean. No one dared to cross his path, especially after what had happened just a few minutes ago. As he walked down the lane, Kirti came running to him from behind.

"Sir… Sir!!"

"Kirti, I want search parties looking for Shelly across the globe right now. And…"

"Sir...That's a shot in the dark. We will never find her. He sent her through a portal. All we could know is that she might be hovering over in distant space."

"No no no...She is here. I know. Didn't you hear what Advik said? 'Sail with the forgotten,' that's a sea, an ocean. Send every troop in the seven seas and track her watch. Maybe we can find her with that. Advik may seem indifferent, but he isn't cruel enough to kill a person. What astounds me more is his way of pursuing things. He seems different, amending, more than capable of just creating portals..."

"Sir that's what I wanted to tell you."

"What do you mean?"

"See this."

Kirti passed the tab to NAT that changed his expression from a worried man to a terrified human being.

"Catastrophe!!! When?"

NAT expressed in a very serious and disturbed tone.

"We are yet to find out sir...but without Dr Shelly's help, it's strenuous," Kirti replied.

"Hmmm...! Did you find Advik?"

"Yes sir! Our satellites picked him up in the Sahara Desert. He keeps on changing his location every five

minutes throughout the globe. Macao, Sydney, Denmark, Mongolia, Sahara… now Himalayas", Kirti quoted.

"I want him seized and unharmed. Send Master, NOW!"

Tense and concerned, uncle NAT ordered Kirti for my return. But little did he know that it was the least dangerous problem right now. Kirti nodded and left immediately as NAT walked back in his cabin.

CHAPTER 7

Good Intruders

(After Advik left the secret base of VPRO in the South Atlantic Ocean.)

As soon as I left the lab I travelled beyond the sea and sand to search for my mother's butcher. From Indian seas to American deserts, from Arctic Circle to the Bermuda Triangle, every place I stood, my eyes searched for him. Although being this 'new being' gave me an upper hand of seeing far beyond the seas, my search was as dry as dust. After an hour of searching the entire globe, I came back disappointed and dejected to the one place that held a special yet aching place in my heart; the place where my mother died, my home. I came back with only one hope that he might have returned here either out of regret or out of impudence.

In comparison to the other neighboring houses, my house looked older and more decrepit. Nevertheless, being back home made me feel calm and nostalgic. As soon as my feet touched our yard, my legs trembled and I kneeled. My heart felt heavy and my eyes kept on searching for answers. *"Why Dad? Why?"*

I was back to normal as I entered the house. The first corner I deliberately wanted to see was my parents' room; hoping one of them or both might still be there; but there was just a void. Everything was the same; nothing was different, just dark and abandoned.

There was this white but a bit dusty lab coat lying on the bed, the same one my mother wore the last time she stepped into this room, the last time she was in this house. It hadn't moved since she left, like it was still waiting for her to come back. I took the coat in my hand, wore it and felt my mother's warm hug in it. The coat still had her rosy smell which made me feel that she was right there with me. It was the only thing I had left of hers and I didn't want to take it off. I hung on to it for a while and let my tears out. As I was mourning my loss, I heard a sound coming from downstairs. I ran towards it to witness someone sitting on the same chair my mother died on.

I knew it could not be my mother as it was a man's butt printing the chair, and my father wouldn't dare to come here after what he did, then *who was he*?

The guy was wearing some kind of armor painted in dark colours. Half of his face was covered with some kind of mask from forehead till his nose. He carried a stylish grey beard and messy hair on top. He sat on the chair as if he owned it, admiring his large shiny sword that even twinkled in the dark. It made me uncomfortable and noxious.

"Little momma's boy, done crying? Did you not get your allowance? Oh right! Who will pay you now?" He mocked.

His bitter words angered me but not enough to change me into the vicious monster like before. I still didn't know how these powers work. Rest assured it was out of my control. Fist tight, I asked for his introduction and purpose of desecrating my place of memories.

"Believe me, you won't like knowing me. And as far as the purpose is concerned, we are here to take you back where you belong."

Saying that, he got up, kept his huge sword on his right shoulder and stepped in the light of the setting sun that peeked from the broken window.

"WE!!?" I curiously asked because other than him there was no one else around to justify the "we".

Before I could understand, out of nowhere, from a dark corner, a woman appeared with a silky curve. She looked completely dim. As dark as the mind of a comedian. Not to sound racist, but she was so gloomy that I was unable to recognize her. The only part I could make out of her was the curves of her body and her deep white eyes with no pupils in them. The woman looked like a living silhouette with two beautiful eyes.

I sharply replied, *"I am where I belong. Get out before you face the consequences."*

My eyes became deep dark like space and my voice a bit heavy. The third time, I was able to understand my powers a bit better but I was still unaware of its limitations and what triggered them to activate. They took a step towards me crushing my mom's flowers that were now dried and converted to dust. I floated up and turned into the very being people feared. Seeing me fly they both stopped stunned for a second. Either they underestimated me or were very presumptuous from the beginning. The guy with the sword stood in defense with his sword and a gun that came out of nowhere, while the woman just stood there fearlessly looking at me, as if she was mesmerized. I didn't want them to impair my home so I carried them away in an open field through a wormhole. We weren't far from home. Actually, it was an old playground where I used to play with my father, and mom used to enjoy watching us getting along.

As the setting sun's ochre light carved my shadow on the overgrown grass 10 feet below me, I warned them one last time to leave me alone. But all I got in return was gunfire. I saved myself like before in the lab but the guy was persistent to shoot me down. I was ten feet above the ground and 100 meters away from him. Surprisingly, he aimed well with no slip. Yet what distracted me the most was that woman who continued to stare at me like a greedy fox.

Nevertheless, I kept defending myself from what was coming but that guy stopped at nothing. It amazed me how many weapons he carried without getting noticed, because as soon as his current gun used to run out of ammo, he used to change to a bigger one out of nowhere. In the middle of all this, he caught my leg once with a whip as I flew like a jet above him but I cut it out with a small hole that appeared in between the whip. There was no opening for me to counter-attack. All I did was defend myself and hear him give a shout to his partner. Being this new person was like being in a dark box with lots of holes in it. I could see what was happening but was bound to something to stop it. The joystick was not in my hand but something inside me was driving it like crazy.

"Shadow? Shadow!!! What are you doing there?"

He shouted out loud while trying to pierce me with his daggers. But Shadow stood still leering at me.

I felt a little drained out because of it, as if someone was sucking out my soul, drop by drop. I was irked with his non-stop firing, and running, and hiding; so I opened up a hole which shot millions of small pebble-like asteroids at them. The guy with the sword took cover but the shadow girl stood still, unaffected. In fact, the meteoroids phased through her hitting the ground.

"What are you?" I whispered.

Here the sword man finally acknowledged that bullets weren't the answer to my wormhole so he ran towards me blocking every meteoroid just with his sword. I closed the meteoroid hoop once he passed by it and I created another wormhole right below his feet thinking he would fall in it. Like a puddle he thought that he could just jump over it but as he was above the hole, the wormhole's gravity tried to suck him in.

"SHADOW!"

His yawp broke her focus off me. Shadow saw what was happening and she swept right between him and the wormhole like a black silky cloth flying in the air and they both disappeared.

I was stunned to see someone do something like that, ironically, as I do it too. I tried to find them beyond seas. From India, I gazed all over to the heights of the Himalayas, to every speck of sand in

Egypt, and to the depths of Sri Lankan forests, but I just couldn't find them anywhere. I closed the wormhole and slowly landed on the ground being Advik. My shadow stretched behind me as the sun went down slowly. Amazed as I was, I felt relieved that they were gone.

"A sword to defeat me?"

I smirked as I felt a bit of pride in me. The very thought that the wormhole gulped them both into the vast space made me feel happy. Then all of a sudden, a voice came from behind me. As I turned to see who it could be, my chest felt a 1,000-volt shock that travelled through my entire body without giving me any chance to turn back into the powerful being.

"Right! A taser could have worked."

It was that guy with the sword who mocked me as I lied on the ground. My own shadow betrayed me as the 'Shadow girl' emerged with that sword man through my silhouette and surprised me from behind.

My eyes flickered on and off like a dying robot as my powers tried to surface. But they didn't.

"DAD"

I said in a cracking voice looking through the sky. I passed out.

CHAPTER 8

The Falling Star (part 2)

(12 hours later on an abandoned island.)

(May 19th, 2035. 12:40 AM)

The sky turned dark and silent. It was the night when the moon disappears and the sea leaves the shore vacant. Shelly washed up to an island before nightfall, unconscious. It was late night and she still wasn't back in her senses. She lay on the beach like a dead person until a cold breeze touched her wet body and gave her the chills. Shelly slowly opened her eyes to witness the twinkling knights of the night. She felt happy feeling a land beneath her. Shelly quickly got up with excitement but felt a lot of ache in her body, especially in her arms and legs. But she had to get up to warm herself, otherwise the cold night might kill her soundlessly. She looked around the island but no one seemed to be nearby. Shelly thought of shouting for help but she knew that would grab the attention of the wild life too, if there were any, so she kept quiet.

Everything was dark and gloomy. Shelly stood up on a cold and abandoned beach. Behind her was a dark mysterious forest and ahead of her laid a vast sea of disappointment. She had nowhere else to go but rest where she stood right now. In the dark, she gathered some raw wood from around the edge of the forest to create a warm surrounding. Sitting by the fire, she tried to locate the human heartbeat she previously tracked but her watch had dried out.

"Great…! I guess I will have to wait till the morning to charge this...", she said in discontent.

Cuddling herself, she slept on the dry, cold sand nearby the fire.

Next morning, Shelly started her struggle for survival. With still a lot of pain in her hand, Shelly collected some weeds for ache, some wood, and some edibles from the edge of the jungle. She never entered the forest to its deepest, just till a particular point from where the sea and the camp were clearly visible. Her elder sister was a botanist so Shelly had some knowledge about healing leaves and weeds.

She left her watch on charge in the sun and wandered nearby the forest for some sign of a human for help. Shelly also set up a camp on the beach and created a soft bed out of leaves. After applying a lotion made out of weeds, Shelly started collecting stones to create a huge SOS sign on the beach.

Later that afternoon, as Shelly was making the sign nearby, her watch beeped. It was fully charged and ready to operate. Shelly excitingly ran towards it as fast as she could with her aching legs. She tried to contact the base again through the watch but it was out of reach. She then tried tracking the human heartbeat she had gotten before. The heartbeat came from here, this island. She was at the right place. Shelly had never felt so happy and relieved about anything. The signals were coming from the deepest part of the forest. She thought of reaching out to whoever it was but the place was unfamiliar and dangerous for a wounded person. She was unprepared for any kind of threat. Moreover, it was too late to start such an unreliable mission.

The twilight commenced with grace. From blue to orange to black, the sky changed its color in a blink of an eye. Shelly built a fire to fight the cold night. It had been 35 hours since she had been separated and there was yet no sign of a living being. Of course, the watch tracked a human heartbeat but how much can we rely on technology? Shelly ate what she could find and drifted off in peace, pushing all her pain and agony on tomorrow.

The next day was crucial for her. She had to pass through the unknown to search for someone whom she hasn't even met before. She had her lab key on a keychain which also possessed a mini multi-purpose tool kit. Shelly used that kit to make a spear out of a staff that she found nearby. She was scared to enter the forest and face the risks but this was her only choice. She prepared herself for everything. Yet her heart was not prepared for entering the darkest place where the wild lived among the shadows of barbarically swirled trees.

The woodland gave an unnerving vibe even in the brightest daylight. Shelly gazed towards the forest for a while. Her mouth felt dry already. As soon as she decided to take a step in, her legs froze. She sweated nervously and stood still until she heard a roar. She ran away from the forest as soon as she heard it.

"What the bloody hell was that…Fuck it…I… I'm not going in there. I am a scientist for God's sake, not Tarzan's girlfriend," she said to herself in a shaky voice.

"If someone truly is inside there, then he or she has to come finding me."

Saying that, Shelly started collecting as many raw woods and sticks as possible to create a huge smoke.

The day ended unproductively and so did the week. Each day Shelly checked the signal, gathered her courage to enter the forest, and every day a current flowed down her spine and scared her away. Anomalously, the signal never moved from its original place ever. She kept the fire running day and night in a loop but nothing was achieved through it. No one ever came looking for her, neither from the forest nor from the sea beyond.

"Wow! And I thought humanity was still alive!"

She said in a very frustrated and upsetting way with a hint of sarcasm and disappointment in it.

The very next morning, Shelly packed some essentials and grabbed her spear to enter the forest. In this entire week of waiting, Shelly had carved a bottle out of a wooden log and a carry bag out of banana leaves. She stood at the entrance of the forest, staring at it agitatedly.

"Okay Shelly, this is it. This is your only choice. You have nowhere else to go but inside. I can't be stranded on this beach anymore… I will have to face my fear…,"

She encouraged herself, took a deep breath to ease her mind and entered the forest once and for all.

At first, she was frightened and reacted even to the slightest noise that she heard but later on, she started seeing its beauty and embraced it. She regretted not visiting the forest any sooner because now that she was here, it wasn't that bad at all. Sighting various birds and witnessing beautiful scenes, Shelly started focusing on her mission. The signal came right from the middle of the island.

As she went deeper and deeper to the centre of the forest, the temperature started to drop gradually. She was near her destination now. She could feel it.

She ran towards the centre of the forest, screaming and shouting in excitement. As Shelly reached her course she was shocked to see no signs of any human beings. No hut. No person, no shattered trees, no garbage lying around.

"But...But, how could this be?!!!"

She checked her watch again and again, but it still showed the same heartbeat right where she stood. She felt very strange and spooky. As she was lost in her thoughts, she heard the cracking sound of dry sticks nearby. Shelly became cautious. She looked around but all she could see was the trees, the jungle and thousands of eyes staring at her from the dark. The thought of being the only person in the forest scared her again and she started to hallucinate.

It was late to travel out now. The sun was slowly sinking in the sea. Shelly started to panic. As she was putting herself together she saw a cave nearby. Shelly ran towards it without wondering what might be inside it. The night started getting colder and scarier every minute. Shelly lit up a fire in the cave and started weeping.

It was three in the morning, the cave was abandoned and was no home to anybody, or at least that's what she thought until she heard a sound from the cave's darkest corner. As she wiped her eyes to see clearly she saw two red eyes staring at her from the dark. Shelly got so scared that she wasn't even able to move a muscle. Slowly the eyes started moving towards her. She covered her eyes and accepted her end. But her luck might be at its best as it was just an owl in the dark. The owl flew away but helped Shelly discover that there was more to the cave than it being just a shelter. She picked up a lit stick and moved towards the dark. The path had no end to it. She kept walking and discovering the huge cave.

As she went deeper and deeper, she felt cold and shiverish. Shelly noticed that the walls were covered with ice. She kept walking the only path until she found an end. After a while of walking, Shelly found out that the cave had a secret tunnel that led to something that she had never expected to see in her entire life. Another cave beneath the island covered with cold icy snow. She was amazed to see something like this above the equator. But then again, the island always gave her a weird vibe. She solved the mystery of the cold she felt in the forest and the enigma of the human heartbeat. It was standing right in front of her.

The cave was as cold as a human heart could be, and in that cave was a humongous creature right in front of her. He stood taller than four humans together. His hands were long enough to scratch his knees without bending. His barbaric structure gave Shelly the chills. The creature belonged to the oldest civilization, maybe the first civilization of humankind. But more than being scared Shelly was stunned and fascinated to study him. The being was trapped in ice for a very long time which gave Shelly a sense of relief.

"Ohhhhh! It's you whose heart has been beating for me. But for a huge creature like you the heart is too soft," Shelly expressed herself.

She thought for a while touching the ice, *"Maybe the ice is holding you behind but just enough to keep you alive."*

All of a sudden Shelly heard a loud gust outside. She ran towards the sound in no time. The sun peeked above and spread its light all over the kingdom. Shelly came out to witness a thing falling from the sky at a great speed from a great altitude.

The thing hit the sea with a blast. She ran towards the smoke through the jungles till the beach. Shelly felt grateful and joyful knowing that someone was nearby. She wanted to get inside water to greet the person, but the incident took place at a distance.

"Looks like a ship? Or is it a satellite? What is it?" she questioned her vision.

Shelly created a fire and tore a piece of her lab coat to wave it like a flag to grab the attention of the pilot or any crew member. Half an hour passed by but Shelly saw no signs of a person or a boat swimming towards the shore. She felt that something was wrong. Shelly threw the flag and dived in to swim a thousand meter with just one thought; if she was not able to come across any person then at least she would be able to find some essential goods or better, a communication device. As she was halfway to the ship, she saw some movement. She stopped in the middle to gaze at it, but before she could observe clearly, a portal opened right below her feet and she was flushed out of there.

(Back in the ice cave on the island, the iceberg that was holding the being had now developed a small crack due to the loud blast.)

CHAPTER 9

Pep Talk

(Secret base vessel of VPRO. 4 days after Advik was captured.)

(May 23rd, 2035. 1:00 PM)

I broke out of my unconscious state to find out that I was in a huge grey lab with only one doctor assisting me. This time I was not in any glass tube but on a soft white bed. I slowly started to gain my senses and saw that I was the only one in the huge room who was being treated. My head felt heavy. Everything was moving until a doctor gave me an injection.

"Don't worry. You are safe now. Rest easy,"

She said in a sweet, lovable voice as she injected me with something.

I slowly fell asleep.

(2 days later after a quiet sleep.)

(May 25th, 2035. 6:37 PM)

I gradually opened my eyes. I was still in the same bed, in the same room, but alone, with no one around me. After a very long time, I had a good sleep. After a very long time, I had felt this quiet. But my peace was not accepted by few people. As I sat back up on the bed, some doctors and security barged in. A few pairs of eyes peeked through my soul, amongst which I noticed a very familiar one. It was the same doctor who had injected me and had stood against Shelly for me, Dr. Kirti. I didn't have a clear glimpse of her that day, but now that I did, it made me feel butterflies in my tummy.

Dr. Kirti was a young assistant to Dr. Shelly, and an astonishingly beautiful bright young girl, with cute little round spectacles on her petite nose. Her hair curled down like a chocolate river and was as brown as her eyes could be. Her lips were as soft and red as a cherry. One might as well take a bite a poisonous apple and sleep for eternity to taste it once. She was the youngest amongst all. Maybe even younger than me but she stood a little taller with a white overcoat hanging on her smouldering sultry physique.

Kirti came forward and asked me how I felt but before I could answer, the devil in the room appeared, NAT. He came in wearing a lab coat and stood at a distance facing me. I didn't like seeing him around, so I turned around and showed my back. I didn't have anything to do with a person who impersonated my mom just to get through me.

"Why are YOU here?"

I asked in a very rude and insensitive voice.

"I am here... to apologize... for my behaviour earlier",

He said in a very calm and regretful voice.

"Then just do it and leave," I said frustratingly.

NAT ordered everyone to wait outside and took a step forward towards me after they left.

"You were pinned below the heavy pile of rocks after the explosion...after the evacuation of the building, I was just a mile away...unaware... when it happened... Something... flew towards me at that time...and landed right near my feet...It was your cycle's seat...Terrified I ran to the explosion just to make sure you were alright...my heart...stopped pumping seeing you in pain...you were crushed and bathing in the pool of your own blood... Rods pierced your bones...all the way through, anchoring the ground...Yet you had few breaths left in you. Somehow, I put myself together and tried to save you...there was no one around to help...And I knew that no one would come...I somehow managed to lift the burden off your back and took you to the hospital...I was not ready to lose my friend and my

only son on the same day...You were critical and later slipped into a coma...I burst into tears seeing you like that...I was afraid to face Maya...But I had to...I reached your house Advik, to inform your mother but she was long gone...My heart stopped thrice in a single day...I cremated your mom and performed the rituals as you were in a deep sleep...in a single day I lost everything...You are my only family left, Advik...and I cannot even imagine hurting you...What I did earlier was just to calm you and not to hurt you... But I am sorry if I did," NAT expressed himself, in a crumbling voice, shedding tears.

I too was not a stone-hearted person. As he dripped tears soundlessly, I too cried remembering everything that had happened.

"It's okay if you don't accept it. I did my part. Just one request, please bring back Shelly or at least tell me where you sent her. She is a very valuable asset and we can't afford to lose her, not now at least. If you do this, I will assume that you have accepted my apology."

I stood my ground, not looking at him and showcasing my weakness. He left with disappointment which was visible in his walk. The security went with him leaving two of them behind, just in case. Kirti and other doctors entered and started to treat me.

Later that night, I couldn't get myself to fall asleep. NAT's words bounced around my head like millions of crazy balls against the walls. I was good enough to walk around the room, so I did that to clear my head. I tried watching some TV and reading the comics, which Kirti had left me with for my entertainment but nothing grabbed my attention. I felt sorry for my actions towards NAT. He had nothing to do with what had happened with me. Uncle NAT had always tried to protect me as his own child. I felt bad for disrupting our relationship. Since I was his only family now, so was he to me. Dawn arrived with a smile. Sleep didn't pass by me that night. As I was sitting near the window peeking at the sea beyond and hearing the calm tide, Uncle NAT came by.

"I promised you that I would help you control your powers, even though I was pretending to be someone else, it's my duty to fulfill it. Once you are able to control your abilities and live with it, you will be free to go…anywhere you want," Uncle NAT said in a serious and responsible tone.

"Come with me," he insisted.

I was still gazing at the beauty of nature.

As uncle NAT was about to leave, I said,

"Mom used to always say…that I am special…I am her special child…but she never told me being special comes with a price."

A tear dropped as I looked at uncle NAT. He couldn't feel more sorry for me. I wiped the tears from my cheeks and slowly stood up. I turned into the being everyone was afraid of and created a portal to bring back Shelly. Within seconds Dr Shelly was flushed inside the room with lots of water and fish. Her clothes were torn and wet. She seemed wild and cranky. She looked at me with her red eyes, don't know what caused them, the anger or a sleepless night. I came back to my original form and avoided any eye contact with her. I felt guilty.

"NAT! In my cabin, now!"

Shelly shouted as she passed by him to the exit.

"Shelly, what happened? Are you okay?"

NAT expressed his concern.

Shelly looked at him angrily and NAT's gibberish stopped in a second. I certainly came to know who was the boss here. I smiled and got back to enjoying my view as they left.

CHAPTER 10

Catastrophe

(Thereafter, in Shelly's cabin.)

"Shelly, I am so, so, so, sorry for what happened to you, but you gotta understand, Advik might seem like an adult now but from inside he is still a child,"

NAT explained to Shelly.

"Nat... Nat... NAT", she shouted to make a point.

"It's okay... I am past it", she said calmly while looking for her spare clothes.

"Actually...I am not...but that's not the point right now...I have something very important to tell you", Shelly said excitingly.

"What is it?" NAT asked.

Shelly very excitingly and animatedly told everything about what had happened to her, to NAT, what she saw after being transported by Advik, and so on.

"No jokes! Are you serious? Where is it?"

NAT asked out of shock and curiosity.

"That's the problem. I don't know... It could be anywhere, any island on this earth," she said cluelessly.

"Then I suppose we need to find it. And we need to find it before you-know-who," NAT said after thinking for a while.

They both sat on their chairs thinking, after Shelly asked *"How?"*

Shelly was still in those wet clothes. Some things were much more important than the feel of dry, fresh clothes. After a while, she got up and started walking around the room, thinking and wetting the floor.

"How about we ask Advik himself?" Shelly suggested.

"NO... no... he is already coping with a lot of things; plus, I want to involve as minimal amount of people in this as possible," NAT said rejecting her idea.

They both started to think over it again. The water droplets dripping from Shelly's clothes made NAT anxious but that was the clue.

"Your clothes. You...your clothes. That's it," NAT expressed excitingly and got up.

Confused, Shelly asked,

"What about my clothes?"

"Remove them," NAT said excitingly taking a step towards her.

NAT's action made Shelly uncomfortable. Who wouldn't be? We look twice before stripping in our own bathroom and he is asking her to do that in front of him very bluntly and blatantly.

"WHOA...WHOA...WHOA! Back off pervert! This is so unprofessional and highly inappropriate of you. That is not how you approach a woman. Plus, this is not the right time. I expected better from you," Shelly

said to NAT, disgusted and disappointed. It took a while, but NAT understood Shelly's reaction and took a step back.

"Oh! No! No, No, No, No, No, No, No,...NO! I didn't mean that. I am sorry but what I was trying to say is that the water, dust, sand particles and other things that came along with you on your clothes can help us find out where you were these past eight days," NAT explained his actions.

"That's right. OMG! You are a genius,"

Shelly exclaimed in excitement. As the conversation was going on, Kirti entered trying to find NAT.

"Sir! Advik is waiting for you in the training arena," Kirti informed sincerely.

"Oh! Great. Kirti, I have a job for you. Take Dr. Shelly's clothes to the lab and examine every particle, every drop of water to determine where it is from and head back to me with the results ASAP. We need to know where Shelly was till now. It's important. Put it on the top priority list."

Saying that, NAT left the room leaving an awkward silence behind. Shelly asked Kirti to lock the door for her and started changing into fresh new clothes. Shelly took the initiative to clear the mist of awkwardness with a taunt.

"I see you think you are more knowledgeable than me," Shelly said in arrogance.

"I am sorry?"

Kirti expressed, clueless about what Dr. Shelly was talking about.

"You chose to reject my orders earlier and run away. You think I didn't notice that? And plus, you reported me to NAT. So tell me, did the ass-kissing get you my job?" Shelly said after changing her clothes.

Kirti was shocked at Shelly's allegation. She knew Shelly was an arrogant, heartless and bit of a pain-in-the-ass kind of person, but she never thought Shelly could be a competitive bitch who was insecure about her position.

"Wha...What? I reported you not for the position but because you were trying to kill Advik," Kirti anxiously and angrily expressed.

It was natural of her to do so. The person you have been with for so long and worked hard without caring about day or night; it was surprisingly unacceptable to hear something like this from them.

"I am the head of the only medical department in this vessel with more experience than your age. I know what I am doing when I am doing it," Shelly raised her voice to prove her point.

She was hurt by Kirti's behaviour and was not ready to forgive her at any cost.

"The circuits that were attached to the button were directly commanding the intravenous lines punctured in Advik's body and brain. Pushing the button would have killed the flow of energy and we would have been left with a dead body," Kirti agitatedly expressed as a counter argument.

"NO! It would have not," Shelly said.

"That would have happened IF he was still inside the pod. After coming out from the pod, the IV lines were only damaging his brain. This would have first led to headache, then hallucination, then nosebleed and in the end, brain hemorrhage," Shelly continued and proved herself right.

Kirti realized her mistake. She was shocked, stunned to know that her decision was going to kill someone. She sat on the chair nearby feeling guilty and ashamed. She felt like a deceiver to Shelly. Shelly was Kirti's only teacher and mentor; and she felt bad doubting her decisions.

"It's alright. You did what you felt right,"

Shelly said egoistically but pitying her simultaneously, and sat on her chair.

"Now I will do what's right for me,"

She took a dramatic pause and continued,

"You are hereby demoted from your rank and position as my assistant for failing to support, accept, and comply with a direct order from your senior... From now on, you will be working in the ER for the next one year, until you learn to be an obedient and supportive team player."

Saying that, Shelly threw her previous clothes for the lab test towards Kirti and asked her to leave. Kirti was shocked to hear this from Shelly but she knew that she deserved it. She took the clothes and got up to leave.

"If we have a year..."

Kirti muttered disappointedly and was about to leave, when Shelly stopped her to ask why she said that.

"Advik has PCS, Preversal Cerebral Syndrome," Kirti replied.

Shelly was shocked to hear that as she had not expected it as an outcome of Advik's independence. Kirti continued,

"As we know, his brain worked slower than his age from birth. But since he has woken up from the long nap, it has started working as well as aging faster than ever. Right now he might be 20 years old and his brain might be that of a 10-year-old child, but it will keep on upgrading every day - ***each day like a month****. If we don't find a way to stabilize his brain now, then his brain will die even before his body can age. And if this*

happens, his body will soon turn into a massive black hole which will be capable enough to gulp in the entire Milky Way."

"CATASTROPHE!!! You have got to be kidding me,"

Shelly got up slowly in shock as Kirti showed her the reports on the tab.